How To ⌐. Away

With Murder

Evil Masterminds Who Evaded

Capture

Roger Harrington

How To Get Away With Murder: Evil Masterminds Who Evaded Capture

'Getting away with murder' is a phrase which gets thrown around regularly. By modern terminology, it means to go unpunished for a crime which requires some sort of correction. It is generally used metaphorically; i.e. in regards to a minor incident which is then sensationally overblown; it is rarely a term used literally.

However, there are circumstances in which the phrase rings true. There are indeed real life instances of criminals who got away with murder - so who are they? What crimes did they commit? How did they evade capture?

There appears to be two types of situations in which one can be said to literally get away with murder. The first, and most common, is that the killer remained unknown until his criminal activity stopped. The second is that the killer was apprehended and tried, but was found innocent due to lack of evidence, loopholes in the justice system, or some other type of underhanded tactic.

The cases which follow are all instances in which a perpetrator of a horrific crime evaded capture and continued to live their lives without repercussion. For each case, the actual truth is entirely unknown, and there exists the very real possibility that the killer (or killers) were imprisoned, died or suffered a similar deserved fate once their crimes ceased.

Part 1 – Zodiac Killer

If not for the looming shadow of Jack the Ripper, the Zodiac killer would perhaps be the most high-profile uncaptured criminal to ever be known to the world. Every aspect of the Zodiac's profile indicated a murderer whom was almost fictional in his characteristics. His murders were brutal and unforgiving. He targeted young couples and was remorseless in his approach. He taunted the police with letters, phone calls and cryptic clues as to his identity, and while police believed they were incredibly close to catching him, they nevertheless failed to do so.

San Francisco, California. The Zodiac Killer's crime spree began on 30th October 1966 when an 18-year-old student named Cheri Jo Bates was discovered dead in her vehicle outside Riverside City College library.

On first glance, there appeared to be motive to this attack. Nothing was stolen from Bates and there was no indication of rape. Bates' cause of death was due to a knife attack to her throat which a pathologist would later claim was so deep it almost decapitated her. After this fatal wound, Bates was strangled, beaten and stabbed across the face several more times.

Initially, police assumed this attack to be a one-off. Forensic signs later determined that Bates and the killer had spent over an hour together in Bates' vehicle before the attack had occurred, suggesting Bates knew her killer well enough to welcome him into her vehicle without hesitation. This is a plausible theory, however, later attacks escalated the

Zodiac's crime spree to strange new heights which disregard this possibility.

Around six month after the death of Cheri Jo Bates, a letter was sent to the press, police and even Bates' father with the message: "Bates had to die. There will be more". Considered to be genuine by authorities, each letter was scoured for fingerprints but no successful matches were found.

The Zodiac's next kill would come on 20th December 1968. Young couple David Arthur Faraday and Betty Lou Jensen were parked in their car overlooking Lake Herman when cream-coloured Chevrolet parked up directly behind them. Within seconds, the driver of the Chevrolet had exited his vehicle, walked up to Faraday and Jensen's car and began shooting at them.

Forensics believed that the Zodiac began shooting at the couple's vehicle from behind, taking out its windshields and tyres, and eventually Faraday with a single bullet to the head. Jensen exited the vehicle in terror and attempted to run, however she was shot down around thirty feet from her car.

As soon as the couple had been killed, the Zodiac left the crime scene. He did not wait around to commit post-mortem mutilation or attempt to cover his tracks in any way. Again, no rape or burglary was evident, which made a motive difficult to establish.

It would be six months before the Zodiac would strike again, this time in the parking lot of Blue Rock Springs Golf Course. 5th July 1969 – in a manner similar to the previous Zodiac victims, a young couple – Darlene Elizabeth Ferrin and Michael Renault

Mageau – were approached by an unknown assailant as they sat in their cars.

Again, the killer pulled up directly behind them. He exited his car and approached Ferrin and Mageau whilst holding a torch or flashlight, to which the couple assumed the assailant to be an undercover police officer. As he approached them, his pulled a gun from his inside coat pocket and fired rounds at Magaeu. Due to the close range from which he fired, the pellets ricocheted from Magaeu's flesh and entered Ferrin. As Ferrin tried to escape, he shot her in the back, leaving both victims wounded inside their vehicle.

Mageau would go on to survive the attack due to emergency medical assistance arriving shortly after the attack. Ferrin, however, unfortunately did not survive. She was pronounced dead shortly after the attack.

A few weeks later, on July 31, 1969, the San Francisco *Examiner*, San Francisco *Chronicle*, and Vallejo *Times-Herald* all received letters in which the author claimed responsibility for the previous attacks. More bizarrely, however, was the attached cryptogram which the author had sent.

Genuine consideration was given to the authenticity of the letters, largely due to the intimate knowledge of each murder the author possessed; knowledge which wasn't published by newspapers at the time.

The cryptogram was published in each paper, and was solved a week later by a high school professor and his wife. However, despite the claims which came with the puzzle, the deciphered message did not reveal the identity of the Zodiac Killer. Translated without spelling errors (likely unintentional), the message the killer claimed:

"I like killing people because it is so much fun. It is more fun than killing wild game in the forest, because man is the most dangerous animal of all. To kill something is the most thrilling experience. It is even better than getting your rocks off with a girl. The best part of it is that when I die, I will be reborn in paradise and all that I have killed will become my slaves. I will not give you my name because you will try to slow down or stop my collecting of slaves for my afterlife."

Multiple letters were then sent to the police over the next few months, many of which were considered to be genuinely sent by the killer. It is in these subsequent letters that the author refers to himself as the Zodiac; many of his letters began with *"This is the Zodiac speaking"*.

The next attack would come on 27th September 1969, three months after the murders of Darlene Elizabeth Ferrin and Michael Renault Mageau.

Cecelia Ann Shepard and Bryan Calvin Hartnell, two college students who were picnicking on the shore of Lake Berryessa in Napa County. Shepard noticed a man who did not look out of the ordinary lingering around near where they were sitting. At one point, the man hid behind a tree, despite Shepard having already seen him.

Shortly after, the man emerged from the trees, and was wearing a very unusual mask. It was a hood-type piece of clothing which was square in design, similar to an executioner's hood from the middle ages. Embroided onto the hood was a small circle design which had previously appeared on the letters sent to the authorities as well as the infamous cryptogram send to the press. This logo, it seems, had become the Zodiac's signature.

The killer approached Shepard and Hartnell and first demanded money and their car keys. He told them that he "wanted to go to Mexico". Hartnell handed across everything he had, including his car keys.

Hoping to calm the killer down, Hartnell offered to help him in any way he could. The killer then told Shepard to hogtie Hartnell with some rope he had brought with him. Shepard did, to which the killer told them "he was going to have to stab them".

The killer stabbed Hartnell six times, and a now-retired police officer confirms a further ten times for Shepard, who succumb to her wounds two days later. Leaving them both for dead, the killer then walked to Hartnell's nearby car and, using a black magic marker, inscribed his signature logo and the dates of his Bay Area attacks on the door.

"Vallejo

12-20-68

7-4-69

Sept 27-69-6:30

by knife"

Less than two weeks after this double-homicide, taxi driver Paul Stine would be murdered at the hands of this elusive killer terrorising the streets of San Francisco.

Stine picked up a passenger at the corner of Mason and Geary Streets in Union Square. After arriving at their destination, Washington and Maple Streets in Presidio Heights, the passenger shot Stine in the right side of the head from point blank range. He then took Stine's wallet, keys and cut out a segment of his shirt before exiting the vehicle.

Two days later, the *Chronicle* received a letter from the Zodiac claiming responsibility for the murder, as well as sending them attached samples of the man's shirt to prove he was indeed the killer.

Throughout many of his correspondence letters with the police up to this point, the Zodiac had made multiple threats to eventually "wipe out a school bus". Initially, investigators assumed this to be an unfounded threat as the Zodiac Killer's *modus operandi* did not suggest he would ever risk such a deviation from his usual method of attack.

So far, the Zodiac had always attacked after sundown on weekends. He only attacked young couples in or near their cars, and always attacked in remote suburban areas with bodies of water nearby. However, if the Zodiac was able to deviate so drastically from this MO by shooting an older (than his usual victim choice) male taxi driver in the middle of a city then the chances of him attacking a school bus became a very real possibility.

Several days after this attack, the Zodiac sent a letter to the police informing them he had already built a "death machine" that he claimed he was going to use to explode a bus. Many researchers interpret this to mean that it was a bomb as opposed to any kind of advanced machinery, however it was a cause for concern because the Zodiac was showing signs of exponential escalation in his murders.

Fortunately, the Zodiac would not be known to kill anyone else. There was a botched kidnapping attempt in San Joaquin County in March 1970 which the kidnapper claimed to be the Zodiac, however the victim – Kathleen Johns – was able to escape. This was also the incident which produced the most accurate photo-fit of the Zodiac to date.

Further evidence that the kidnapper was indeed the Zodiac came in the form of a letter sent to the San Francisco Chronicle several months after the incident. In the letter, the author mentioned that he set fire to the victim's car after she had escaped from it, a fact which was not widely publicised in the media.

More letters subsequently arrived to the police, all of them beginning with *"This is the Zodiac speaking"*, despite no more bodies being discovered, nor did the author make mention of any more victims.

After remaining silent for a number of years, it would not be until 1974 that the Zodiac would resurface. In January of the same year, he sent a letter to the San Francisco Chronicle claiming that the recently-released film *The Exorcist* was "the best satirical comedy he has seen in years". At the end of the letter, he threatened that if his letter wasn't published in the Chronicle newspaper then he would "do something nasty".

Several more letters would arrive over the ensuing months, although none of them took responsibility for any further killings. Instead, the letters focussed on mundane things such as the killer's responses to the articles in the newspaper and expressing his disdain for the types of advertisements they were running. San Francisco police have not received any Zodiac correspondence since 1974.

Judging by what we know of the Zodiac's crimes, the perpetrator can be deemed by FBI classifications as an organised offender. What this means is that the Zodiac Killer left his house each evening with the intention of committing murder and came fully equipped with everything he needed to carry out such an attack and escape without leaving any traces of himself behind.

The fact that the Zodiac Killer committed these acts and was able to remove all evidence of his physical presence behind suggests a lot about the perpetrator. Firstly, that he understood, at least to a small degree, law enforcement processes, although this doesn't imply direct connection with law enforcement in any way. It is simply a sign of above-average intelligence and the ability to forward-think. In one letter, the killer made reference to coating his fingertips with cement in order to avoid leaving fingerprints, a further skill which suggests high intelligence scientific know-how.

In the Zodiac's cryptogram, he makes reference to hunting and man "being the most dangerous animal of all". This statement is in contrast with all of the Zodiac's actions because at no point did he "hunt" man. In fact, his actions suggest the opposite. The Zodiac blitz attacked the majority of his victims (besides Cheri Jo Bates – but we do not know much about her murder) which suggests he was unconfident in his ability to control them.

This is further reinforced by the incident at Lake Berryessa in which the Zodiac bound up his victims before stabbing them. This was a major deviation from his usual tactics because he had never restrained his victims previously (or afterwards) and used a knife instead of a gun – at no point was "hunting man" ever implied.

A further strange phenomenon deals with the Zodiac's lack of motive. At times, the Zodiac was known to take the wallets and keys of his victims, but not in every case. If his motive was robbery, he could have taken a lot more items than wallets and keys (it is worth noting that the Lake Berryessa incident, the killer held his victims' keys at one point but chose to leave them at the crime scene).

There was no sexual element to the murders in any way. Sexual gratification is rarely achieved by gunshot and if it was, there would likely have been further evidence to indicate sexual assault. It seems that the only motive available was infamy. In his later messages, the killer asked the media why there hadn't been a movie made about him yet. He also made sure to not take credit for other people's work in one case, suggesting a high level of self-admiration or narcissism.

Throughout the investigation, multiple suspects appeared but all of them were eventually discredited. One suspect in particular, Arthur Leigh Allen, is considered to be the most likely suspect and the one which many researchers believe is the Zodiac Killer.

Arthur Leigh Allen was considered an eccentric outsider by many reports. He was a known paedophile and had complete stints inside mental hospitals due to his recognised illness. He owned several handguns and allegedly kept one in his car at all times. He worked a series of menial jobs throughout his life and by his late thirties (his age around the time of the Zodiac killings), he had isolated himself from most of his friends and family.

The reason Allen became a major suspect, despite there being no evidence to link him to any of the murders, was due to an old friend of Allen's named Donald Cheney coming forward with information. Cheney claimed that Allen mentioned to his idea of committing a series of murders in lovers' lanes throughout the San Francisco area. He allegedly described how he would "use a revolver or pistol with a flashlight attached for illumination and an aiming device, and would walk up and shoot people."

Allen also brought up the topic of the book entitled *The Most Dangerous Game* – a fictional tale of a wealthy man who hunts prisoners on his private island as sport. Although most convincingly of all, Allen also claimed to Cheney he would call himself "Zodiac", stating "I like the name Zodiac, and that's the name I'm going to use."

Despite this, there is very little physical or even circumstantial evidence which points to Allen as a viable suspect outside of Cheney's claims. While Allen was a registered paedophile and made threats towards children in his letters, it is incredibly rare for a paedophile to kill outside of their target group. Furthermore, Allen's handwriting doesn't match any of the letters sent, nor do his fingerprints match any of the prints discovered on the letters.

If Allen was not the Zodiac, which is very likely given the lack of evidence, the question remains: how did the Zodiac Killer avoid detection so well?

The answer lies in a combination of organisation and forensic countermeasures on the killer's part, and lack of DNA profiling methods available to the police at the time. It may have been a perfect storm; an unlikely instance of all of the factors favouring the killer's escape.

There are many theories circulating as to the identity of the Zodiac Killer, even inspiring amateur detectives to this day to attempt to uncover who he really was. Given that the Zodiac crimes only occurred around 50 years ago, it is entirely possible that the killer is still out there today. What is more likely, however, is that the real Zodiac has either passed away or been imprisoned for another crime. The fact he simply disappeared without any kind of sign off indicates that his absence was not his choice.

The crimes of the Zodiac Killer will go down in history alongside those of Jack the Ripper. An elusive mystery forever to remain unsolved.

Part 2 – The Angel of Death: Joseph Mengele

Children liked him. He brought them sweets and drove to their death sites. Joseph (sometimes Josef) Mengele, the Auschwitz physician and ultimate Angel of Death, was perhaps one of the most inhuman monsters to not only ever have lived, but to also have evaded capture.

A leader in the Nazi medical field, Mengele thrived on experiments regarding genetic deformities. Since his crimes came to light, Mengele has come to embody the essence of evil, perhaps because he so willingly violated all professional courtesy in favour of acting out his fantasies of power and control.

Mengele arrived in Auschwitz on May 30, 1943. He was 32 at the time, from a Catholic family, and had been a Nazi supporter since his early years. Mengele was already well-established in the field of medicine, genetic research and surgery, and had specifically requested he be sent to Auschwitz because of opportunities such a place could provide for his research.

As a student Mengele attended the lectures of Dr. Ernst Rudin, who proposed the idea that not only were some lives not worth living, but that doctors had a responsibility to end such life and remove it from existence. Rudin's outspoken ideologies attracted the attention of Adolf Hitler himself, and Rudin was invited to assist in composing the *Law for the Protection of Heredity Health*, which passed in 1933, the same year that the Nazis took complete control of the German government.

In 1937, the two great passions in Mengele's life came to overlap. First, that he craved notoriety as a prestigious scientist. And secondly, that he help towards the genetic purification of an all-Aryan race.

In May of 1938, Mengele applied for membership with and was accepted into the *Schutzstaffel*, or SS. By the age of 28, Mengele had climbed to a place of authority within the Nazi regime and was fated to wield great power and influence over the ensuing years.

The site of Auschwitz was a plague misery and despair. The conditions were appalling. Diseases were rife across the site, with such outbreaks of lice, fleas, vermin and typhus being commonplace. Yet, Auschwitz was where Joseph Mengele reigned.

Mengele's mission at Auschwitz was to perform research on human genetics. His work was funded through a grant that Professor von Verschuer had secured through the German Research Council in August of 1943. His goal was to uncover the secrets of genetic engineering, and to invent methods for eradicating inferior gene strands from the human population.

However, despite this scientific premise, Mengele's did nothing to further the advances of science. Instead, his actions only served to inflict unnecessary cruelty upon innocent children.

Mengele very quickly demonstrated an excessive lust for impulsive murder during a typhus epidemic that broke out in one of the camps shortly after he arrived. Mengele demanded almost one thousand Gypsy men and women who were suffering from the disease directly to the gas chambers.

His lack of hesitation to execute a thousand innocent people without a second thought suggest a cold detachment from his fellow man. Additionally, this is the actions of a man with a dangerous desensitisation to cruelty and death. It is quite clear that Mengele suffered from kind of sociopathic behaviour before being granted a high ranking position within the Nazi regime.

Whatever it was that inspired Mengele to commit this first act of genocide, it continued to fuel his desire to be Auschwitz's premier authority over all matters relating to life and death. Mengele was quickly placed in charge of the "selection" process; the decision as to whether innocent victims lived or died. The process was held after trains carrying Jewish deportees had arrived at the camp, and Mengele's choices were based on personal biases and looks, not any kinds of health check or medical exam. Mengele presided over these selection processes with great enthusiasm; often showing up in his best outfits and clearly enjoying himself deciding other people's fates.

Mengele enjoyed his high ranking position and was entirely comfortable with his responsibly. On the surface, it appeared as though Mengele's motivation for such a task was the racial purification of the human race. He clearly relished the power to yield life and death over such a large amount of people.

If anyone disputed a choice made by an SS officer, Mengele might impulsively beat or shoot them. Mengele appeared to be an inhuman, emotionless monster through the entire process. He showed no conscience and no hesitation, and sent anyone with an imperfection directly to the gas chamber.

Mengele's sociopathic behaviour became clear to anyone who had spent time with Mengele during the selection process. In his efforts to improve the efficiency of the other officers regarding the process, Mengele taught his fellow doctors how to give phenol injections to a long line of prisoners, quickly ending their lives. Mengele also regularly shot people, beat them, humiliated them, and by many reports, even threw live babies into furnaces.

Mengele performed this task with delight, even appearing at selections which he need not officially be present. Despite his obvious pathological need to be detached as well as cruel, Mengele also emitted a grandiose, charming side, which he used to manipulate both colleagues and victims.

He acted in a caring, concerned manner when confronted with exhausted women and their children on the ramp, only to send them to the gas chambers a moment later.

Additionally, Mengele occupied his time with other numerous acts of inhuman barbarism, including the dissection of live children, the removal of children's genitals without the use of anaesthetic, and the administering of electric shocks to women under the guise of testing their levels of endurance.

Mengele would eventually introduce sexual degradation to the already horrific selection process he presided over. Prisoners from the various women's barracks were brought before him and made to strip naked. Mengele would then force each woman to answer questions regarding the intimate details of their sex lives.

Mengele would introduce various substances into the bloodstreams of live children to see what reaction would take place. In most cases, such actions would seriously affect them or kill them. Such occurrences didn't seem to concern Mengele, however, as he believed his supply of victims was endless.

In incredible contrast, even as Mengele singled out these children for experimentation or death, he would play with them and show them, what appeared like, genuine affection. Then, once their death or mutilation had been administered, Mengele would remove their limbs, eyes or organs and attach them to his wall as a trophy.

The most terrifying part, throughout all this, was that Mengele was able to keep a calm, detached demeanour and viewed his actions as beneficial to the progress of science.

Mengele also had one particular obsession: twins. He kept every single set of twins he came across without question. He took great care with them, in stark contrast to how he treated all other children during his selection process. His twins were weighed, measured, and compared to each other in every way. Blood was constantly taken from them and they were questioned extensively about their family histories.

While twins were initially spared from the gas chamber, they were arguably subjected to a crueller fate.

Mengele reserved a special residence for his "children" which he termed the Zoo. These included twins, dwarfs, cripples, anyone with genetic deformities and what he termed "exotic specimens".

As twins were Mengele's favourite subject, they were thusly 'rewarded' with special benefits such as receiving more food than other prisoners and being able to keep their own clothing. Mengele had instructed his colleagues to take extra case if they discovered any sets of twins, as Mengele was reported to suffer outbursts of anger should any of his future specimens come to harm.

Furthermore, Mengele's children were also spared beatings and manual labour in order to preserve their health. However, this was not Mengele's humanity coming into play, it was his desire to keep his specimens healthy for when they came to experimentation. Ironically, it would be the intensity and chaotic nature of Mengele's experiments that caused the children to suffer a death more agonising than one they would have suffered in the gas chamber.

Young children were restrained in cages, and subjected to a variety of chemicals to determine how they might react. Several twins were castrated or sterilized. Many twins had limbs and organs removed in macabre surgical procedures that Mengele performed without using an anaesthetic. Other twins were injected with infectious agents to see how long it would take for them to succumb to various diseases. Mengele even performed some sex-change operations; something was unheard of at the time.

If one twin passed away during his experiments, the other twin was no longer needed. Mengele would then simply send it to the gas chamber.

Mengele had a further obsession with eye colour, and was determined to change the eye colour of his victims to blue. He would attempt to achieve this by injecting various chemicals such as dye, however he failed greatly in his efforts. All of his attempts to change eye colour were met with disease, blindness or death.

Mengele was evidently greatly concerned with the idea of genetic creation of a superior race, however, his personal desires were not lost on his peers. It appeared as though Mengele enjoyed playing God and would continue to do so throughout his entire Nazi career.

The overwhelming evidence against Mengele's guilt is staggering. It is very difficult to categorise Mengele as any type of particular personality disorder due to the combination of circumstances which allowed him free reign to act out his murderous impulses.

Mengele's behaviour evades description. There are multiple theories regarding his motivations, however it is likely that a combination of motivations, fantasies, circumstances, curiosity, eagerness and ambition were the catalyst to such inhuman acts.

First of all, Mengele relished his role as an SS doctor, scientist and researcher. He adhered strictly to his regimented role and abided by the Nazi codes of disciple without question.

We know that Mengele had a need to please his superiors; something which goes entirely against the notion of an experimental sociopath. He continued to keep his mentors updated on his research, whether they were his medical peers or higher-ups in the Nazi regime.

Mengele was reported to have shown cold detachment from his actions, whether they were injecting chemicals into one victim's bloodstream or ordering the deaths of a thousand Jews in the gas chamber. Neither one meant anything to him. Despite this, reports also say that Mengele didn't show pleasure as such, just detachment.

Despite Mengele being an accomplished doctor and scientist, the work he did on the subject of human experimentation discovered no scientific findings whatsoever. Nothing was discovered, and his actions only served to introduce the Nuremberg Code upon the ending of World War II; a series of ethics which must be followed when carrying out experiments.

We can conclude that Mengele's experimentation had absolutely nothing to do with true scientific research; a very strange fact considering Mengele's enthusiasm for scientific discovery. It was simply the result of one man's overly-ambitious adherence to his vision of German supremacy.

Mengele fled from Auschwitz on January 17, 1945. He initially remained in hiding for a number of years, assuming a new identity and working odd jobs as a manual labourer. He kept in touch with German confidantes throughout, who kept him in the know regarding advancements of the Allies and Soviets.

For a while, Mengele attempted to continue his career as a scientist, but he soon realised he would be found out given his obvious occupation, and would be subsequently sentenced to death should he be discovered.

Mengele finally decided that Europe wasn't safe for hiding, and so fled to Argentina via ocean liner in 1949. Fortunately for Mengele, at the time Argentina was ruled by dictator Juan Peron, a noted Nazi supporter and enthusiast. Because of this, Mengele was able to mix in with such a setting quite easily and soon established a new identity thanks to his involvement with multiple Nazi supporters.

Mengele spent the rest of his life evading capture. There were neo-Nazi groups protecting him in South America, but was unknowingly assisted by the lack of co-operation by the German government to locate him.

Mengele's freedom was seemingly overshadowed by the pursuit by authorities to locate Adolf Eichmann, a higher ranking Nazi official who was also rumoured to be living in Argentina. Mengele was close to being captured numerous times by the Israeli government but was able to slip by their cross-hairs every time.

Sightings of Mengele continued through the 1960s and 1970s, with reports of him being located in Spain, Brazil, Paraguay and Greece. Although very soon, Mengele seemed to drop off the radar of all international governments. It wasn't until 1985 when interest in Mengele's whereabouts suddenly reinvigorated.

A group of Auschwitz survivors returned to the death camp in order to pay tribute to those who had died there. The following week, the same survivors gathered in Jerusalem to try Mengele in absentia. The event received extensive media exposure, and for four nights, TV and radio stations were filled with Auschwitz survivors describing their agonising ordeals at the hands of the Angel of Death.

One month later, the United States Justice Department and the Israeli government announced that the case of Joseph Mengele was officially reopened. They were finally going to bring him to justice.

Simon Wiesenthal, a renowned Nazi hunter, stated that he has had the opportunity to capture or kill Joseph Mengele on multiple occasions, but has refrained from doing so. Wiesenthal states his reasons that "Mengele's life is no longer important to us." He claims that killing a man response for 300,000 deaths is futile as it won't bring any about real justice.

On 31st May 1985, German police raided the home of a man named Hans Sedlmeier who was a friend and confidante of Mengele's. The police had been tipped off regarding Mengele and Sedlmeier's acquaintance. Letters between Mengele and Sedlmeier were discovered at the home, and very soon the police were able to track the houses of where Mengele had lived in Brazil.

After thorough investigation, the police discovered that Mengele had reportedly died in a drowning accident in 1979. His death was kept quiet in order to protect those who had sheltered Mengele after his escape from Germany.

The police then discovered the grave where Mengele had been buried in, which possessed the name Wolfgang Gerhard – Mengele's fake name since 1971. The body in the grave was exhumed, and forensic tests confirmed that the skeleton buried inside did indeed belong to Dr Joseph Mengele.

In life, Mengele was the author of life and death. He played god for a number of years and did so without legal or moral repercussion. Mengele was directly responsible for the deaths of around 300,000 individuals, all of whom were killed in a vile, unnecessary, degrading manner. His involvement in such a catastrophic amount of deaths makes him one of the most sought-after criminals ever to have lived, but unfortunately, he will never receive any kind of justice.

Just how Mengele managed to evade capture for over thirty years is unexplainable, particularly as his identity was known to many. It is a tragic state of affairs that he escaped, but Joseph Mengele sought the ability to control life and death, and it turns out he managed to do just that.

Part 3 – The Mad Butcher of Kingsbury Run

"Of all the horrible nightmares come to life, the most shuddering is the fiend who decapitates his victims in the dark, dank recesses of Kingsbury

Run. That a man of this nature should be permitted to work his crazed vengeance upon six people in a city the size of Cleveland should be the city's shame. No Edgar Allan Poe in his deepest, opium-maddened dream could conceive horror so painstakingly worked out..."

Written by a journalist for the *The Cleveland News* in 1938, this seems to sum entirely sum up the legacy of the Mad Butcher of Kingsbury Run.

Sometimes known as The Torso Murderer, the Mad Butcher was an elusive serial killer who operated in Cleveland, Ohio in the 1930s. He was responsible for the deaths of at least twelve people, all of them being mutilated, dismembered and discarded.

September 23, 1935. The day the horrors began. Two police officers were dispatched to a run-down, dilapidated shanty town known to as Kingsbury Run. There were reports that some children had accidentally stumbled across the torsos of two headless bodies.

Sure enough, that's exactly what they discovered. The depravity of which the torsos had been subjected to was beyond comprehension. The two police officers in question reported that they had never seen anything quite like this before.

Two white men, both beheaded, lay strewn between some secluded bushes. Both men had been cleanly decapitated and both had been castrated. Their heads were discovered several meters away in another part of the field. One man had been dead for around three days, whereas the other had been dead closer to ten. Decomposition had begun to set in. Death had been caused by decapitation or blood loss. One man was said to be in his twenties, the other his forties.

Initially, these murders provide a very bizarre type of killer. Firstly, decapitation as a means of death is particularly strange. Decapitation often occurs post-mortem for multiple reasons, and is rare in relation to sexual sadism. Secondly, the fact both victims were twenty years apart in age means he has a broad victim type, making him especially dangerous. Lastly, the time of death between both victims likely indicates that the men were killed elsewhere, at different times, and then disposed of at the same location.

Police confirmed the identity of one victim: Edward A. Andrassy, a 28 year old who had previously worked in the psychiatric ward of Cleveland Hospital. The other victim's identity has never been confirmed.

Eventually, all clues regarding the deaths of both men led to dead ends and the police activity died ceased.

26th January 1936. A third body is discovered. A black woman who had been mutilated was found lying against a building on East 21st Place. Her dismembered body parts were discovered in a bin liner nearby.

The coroner who examined the body claimed that the woman had been dead around three days. Dismemberment was performed with a sharp instrument. As with the previous victims discovered, all incisions made were clean and precise. The killer was likely very knowledgeable regarding butchery or medical procedures.

On 7th February 1936, the rest of the woman' body, with the exception of her head, was found scattered haphazardly against the fence of an empty house. Unfortunately, all leads which could identify the woman dried up.

June 5, 1936. Two young boys had set off to go fishing and took a shortcut through Kingsbury Run. The boys noticed a pair of trousers discarded beneath a bush and when they poked at them with their fishing pole, a man's head rolled out.

Police were alerted and began searching for the body it belonged to. It was discovered the next morning; a bare, headless torso, positioned very close to the police station which the investigating officers worked out of.

It appeared as though the killer was taunting the police.

The body of the man discovered came to be known as 'The Tattooed Man'. The man bore multiple distinctive tattoos which they believed would be help them uncover the man's identity, but to no avail. The tattoos suggested a married man who was possibly a sailor at some point, but again, no confirmed identity was ever discovered.

Coroner's reports believe that this particular victim was not picked up by the killer in the same location as his previous victims. Firstly, the Tattooed Man was well nourished and well dressed, suggesting he was from a different area entirely and was only disposed of in the Kingsbury Run area.

Despite this, the manner of death in which he was murdered was consistent with all other victims. By now, police began to notice a pattern. A serial killer who killed by means of decapitation – a rare, almost-unheard of method of attack in the history of serial killings.

Tales of a psychopathic, elusive madman committing execution-like killings was too good a story for the media to resist. Newspapers ran fictional-like tales of the killer, many of which were based on unfounded rumour and imaginative narratives. The killer come to be known as the Mad Butcher of Kingsbury Run.

July 22, 1936 - Another murder victim was discovered. In the Big Creek area on the southwest side of the city, a teenage girl had found the headless body of a white man. The location she had discovered the body was a notorious spot for homeless people to find shelter.

The body was found naked and lying on his stomach. His head was found a few yards away from his body, wrapped up in the man's clothing. According to coroner's reports, the body had been there around two months before it was discovered.

In contrast to previous victims, it was also found that the man was killed directly in the spot he was discovered. This is a very strange discovery, as it indicates that the killer was able to decapitate a man while he was still alive in a public area. This suggested great physical strength as not only would the killer need to subdue the victim, but also deliver a clean blow to the man's neck in order to decapitate him, all while the victim was alive.

Furthermore, this body was found on the other side of town from Kingsbury Run. It was not transported like the killer's other victims, suggesting he was perhaps interrupted immediately after committing the act and therefore couldn't finish off his fantasy accordingly.

The victim in question was likely a homeless man. He had long hair, was unwashed, had dirty clothing and was discovered in a hobo camp. Additionally, the police were unable to confirm his identity.

10th September 1936. A homeless man who was sitting near E. 37th Street noticed two halves of a human torso floating in the nearby lake. Police immediately arrived at the scene and pulled the torso from the lake. A search was immediately undertaken alongside of the creek and the weeds for the balance of the body.

Morbidly curious spectators gathered around to watch the police drag the pool for the victim's head. Unfortunately, it was never discovered. The victim was found to be a man in his late twenties, but as with the majority of the Butcher's victims, his actual identity was never uncovered.

By modern standards, the police would – by this point – have enough information available in order to make some educated guesses regarding the killer's motivations and his next likely attack. Unfortunately, police techniques were undeveloped at the time and so were unable to form any kind of psychological or physical profile.

It seemed that the killer was playing a game with detectives. The fact he was able to kill in such an insulting manner, leave the bodies near to police headquarters and manage to leave behind no trace evidence was a sign of an accomplished murderer. The police had to up their game in order to catch him.

The police were informed by the lead detective at the time to find the Mad Butcher at any cost. At the time of the murders, infamous law enforcement officer Eliot Ness had been put in charge of the investigation, and his track record of solving cases was being compromised by the Butcher's crimes.

Police officers interviewed anyone who might be related to the crimes in any way, mainly homeless men. Some investigators believed the crimes to contain a homosexual motivation due to the genital castration on some victims, so police scoured gay bars and gay hot-spots for information.

The Butcher would surface again on 23rd February 1937. This would be his seventh victim. The torso was found washed up on the beach at 156th Street, headless and naked. No identity was able to be confirmed, and it would not be until several months later that the remains of the woman would be discovered in the Cuyahoga River.

The most notable aspect of this murder is that the cause of death was not determined to be decapitation, despite decapitation occurring. The removal of the head was likely done after death, which means that the mutilations to the rest of the woman's body were done before prior to decapitation; a deviation from the Butcher's usual MO.

Additionally, and very bizarrely, the killer also inserted a piece of cloth into the woman's rectal cavity. The reasons why have never even been theorised.

On 6th July 1937, the upper section of a man's body floated in the Cuyahoga River near Kingsbury Run. Over the ensuring days, his remains floated downstream until almost his entire body washed up on shore.

Something was strange about the killer's eighth victim: he had removed all of the man's internal organs, along with his heart. These organs were never discovered.

Nine months would pass by before another victim was discovered. On 8th April 1938, a woman's leg was discovered in the Cuyahoga River. Police searched the areas along the riverbank where the leg was found and discovered a burlap sack containing the victims' remains. She had been cut in half, decapitated and severely mutilated.

Two more victims would surface in August of the same year, all bearing the hallmarks of the Mad Butcher. These would be the killer's eleventh and twelfth victims, and luckily for authorities, his last murders. The killings officially stopped in August 1938.

The hunt for the killer continued, but the police had extremely little to go on despite there being twelve known victims. It cannot be a coincidence that of all the victims the Butcher claimed, only two of them were able to be officially identified. What makes matters stranger is that not all of the Butcher's victims were considered to be homeless – some appeared to be normal, healthy working class people – but were still unable to have their identities confirmed.

Because of this, the theories regarding the Butcher's motivations are endless, and in turn this makes a psychological evaluation difficult to ascertain. The killer possesses some form of psychopathy, but was unlikely to be considered insane. The fact that he murdered a man who once worked in a psychiatric ward suggests possible connections with mental health, but his later victims disprove this theory.

There is debate regarding the killer's sexuality given his attention to men's genitals and not women's, but it is likely that sexuality did not come into play in his murders. The broad range of victims (men, women, young, old, white, black) do not imply any kind of sexual connotation and instead point towards a compulsive drive to kill, without a thought as the victim's characteristics.

The Butcher's knowledge of anatomy is more advanced than the common person's, but this doesn't necessarily mean he was directly involved in the medical field. There are multiple professions which lend themselves towards anatomical knowledge, and it is not necessarily indicative of his profession.

There are some things we *can* confirm regarding the butcher, based on all previous evidence. He possessed great physical strength. The fact he was able to carry some victims significant distances as well as cleanly decapitate (one heavy blow is required) them proves this.

The Butcher certainly lived in the Kingsbury Run area. Such a killer would only hunt within territory he was familiar with, especially given his risky taunts towards police. Furthermore, the mess created upon decapitation of a living person would be too much to commit in the open, meaning the Butcher owned his own property. He was not a homeless man like many of his victims.

Popular theories suggest that the Mad Butcher of Kingsbury Run was the same person who committed the murder of Elizabeth Short in 1947. The murder does resemble the crimes, and it is not impossible for this theory to be accurate.

Furthermore, some researchers have suggested Jack the Ripper re-emerged after a forty year hiatus and continued his crime spree in a different country. This is much less likely, although not impossible.

There were a handful of viable suspects throughout the investigation, although none with any concrete evidence to ascertain their involvement with the murders. One particular suspect looked good for the murders – a Dr Francis Sweeney. Sweeney was an accomplished medical official, but was plagued by drink problems throughout his life. Around the time of the murders, Sweeney's wife filed for divorced from him and he lost custody of his children.

Sweeney knew the Kingsbury Run area very well as he grew up there. He was also quite large and physically-capable. Given his profession, he also had the anatomy knowledge in order to successfully cut up bodies and remove organs. Upon Sweeney's interrogation, it came to light that he had slight mental health issues; something unknown to investigators when he was initially considered a suspect.

Eliot Ness went so far as to tell Sweeney outright "I think you're the killer". Sweeney denied these accusations, but then would go on to voluntarily check himself into a mental health facility. The circumstances surrounding this incident is unknown and has never been officially discussed, but what is confirmed is that Sweeney was voluntarily incarcerated as of August 1938. The same month that the killings ceased. Sweeney remained there until his death in 1965.

As with Jack the Ripper and the Zodiac Killer, it seemed that the Mad Butcher of Kingsbury Run was able to evade capture due to a perfect storm of circumstances. Indeed, we cannot discredit his ability to commit murder and leave no trace evidence behind, but if the Butcher were to commit his crimes in the modern age, forensic and psychological advancements would likely be able to eventually uncover the perpetrator. However, the reality is that the identity of the Mad Butcher will be forever shrouded in secrecy. It is safe to say that he has got away with murder.

Part 4 – The Long Island Serial Killer

The cases which we can confirm with certainty that the perpetrator has indeed got away with murder, on the surface, appear to be historical cases from decades past. By now, such cases will be considered 'cold' by authorities, and lack of leads or evidence force the case to be forgotten in favour of newer mysteries.

However, as we speak, there are criminals out there committing crimes which could eventually come to be our generation's Jack the Ripper or Zodiac Killer. One such instance is the Long Island Serial Killer (LISK).

Known by many names (Long Island Serial Killer, Gilgo Beach Killer, Craigslist Ripper), an unknown perpetrator is believed to have killed up to sixteen people over a span of twenty years and discarded their remains in ditches throughout remote town of Gilgo Beach In Long Island, New York.

As recently as 2011, bodies which authorities believe are the handiwork of the LISK have been unearthed. In total, ten bodies have been discovered, all of which are believed to have been committed by a single killer.

On 11th December 2010, police were searching the Gilgo Beach area for a missing woman named Shannan Gilbert. Gilbert, 24, was an escort who used online hub Craigslist to advertise her services. She was last seen around Oak Beach – a community several miles from Gilgo Beach, prompting police to search the surrounding area.

Police didn't find Shannan on that search, but they did find something more alarming. They discovered the skeletal remains of a completely different woman. Her remains had almost entirely perished due to the length of time they'd been there, prompting an immediate investigation.

Two days later, along the same stretch of land, three more bodies were discovered, all bearing similarities in the way the bodies were disposed. The discovery of four bodies all discarded in exactly the same area pointed to the work of a serial killer.

Initially, there wasn't much for the police to go on. They were reluctant to mention that the bodies were the work of a serial killer and kept many details of the bodies under wraps. All they made public was that the victims had been killed and disposed of in a similar manner. All four bodies were discovered in the same quarter-of-a-mile stretch, around 50 yards spaced between each body.

All four victims, so far, were women.

As the investigation went on, more details began to emerge. All victims had been killed elsewhere and disposed of around Gilgo Beach, and the identities of the four victims were made known to the public:

Maureen Brainard-Barnes, 25. A single mother who made her living as an escort. She was last seen in July 2007 in Norwich, Connecticut and was likely also killed around this time.

Melissa Barthelemy, 24. A resident of Erie County, New York who worked as an escort. Last seen in July 2009 before being reported as missing. In the weeks following her disappearance, Barthelemy's sister claims she received bizarre phone calls from her sister's phone, possibly by the killer.

Megan Waterman, 22. Travelled to New York from Maine on 6th June 2010 and was never heard from again. Waterman worked as an escort and was likely travelling to fulfil a client's request.

Amber Lynn Costello, 27. An escort who went missing on 2nd September 2010. According to her conversations, she was due to meet a client that same evening who had offered her a substantial amount of money for her services.

A pattern in the victimology is clearly present. All of the killer's victims were twenty year old escorts who had gone missing around the summer time or slightly after. Additionally, it came to light that all of the victims had been using Craigslist, the same platform as Shannan Gilbert (who had yet to be discovered) to advertise their services.

The case died down around December 2010, despite their clear leads. However, Craigslist favours anonymity due to its lack of procedures to trace conversations. All interactions between members are done between temporary email addresses which are created when a message is sent, and subsequently deleted after several days. By the time the police came to investigate the communication trail, all evidence had been automatically deleted.

Because all of the discovered bodies were wrapped in burlap sacks, some investigators offered the theory that this might be a clue to the killer's profession. However, burlap sacks are regularly used in the construction, food, landscaping and postal trades, which doesn't do much to narrow down suspects.

In April 2011, four more bodies would be discovered by authorities. They were found around two miles away from the first four bodies, and were all discarded in an identical manner. This made a total of eight bodies.

After this shocking discovery, police expanded the search to include Nassau County, a neighbouring suburb to Suffolk County. There, police found an additional body along with partial skeletal remains. In total, ten bodies were discovered, all of whom were attributed to the work of the Long Island Serial Killer.

Only one of the bodies discovered was able to be officially identified. Jessica Taylor, a 20-year-old prostitute whose body was discovered in July 2003 missing its head and hands in New York, was confirmed to have been a victim of the LISK due to parts of her anatomy being discovered along with the other Gilgo Beach bodies. It appears that, somehow, the killer had dismembered Taylor and spread her remains throughout New York.

Amongst the recently discovered bodies, most interestingly, were the remains of a female toddler between the ages of 1 and 2. The toddler's remains showed no signs of injury and was wrapped with a blanket. Furthermore, the remains of the baby's mother would also be found amongst the other bodies.

The remains of the toddler were not the only bizarre discovery in the new mass of bodies. Additionally, one of the bodies appeared to an Asian male who was between the ages of 18 and 23 when he was killed, likely around 2004. He was also found to be wearing women's clothing at the time of his murder.

Speculation regarding the identity of the LISK is widespread, with many different theories being suggested. There are only a handful of facts which can be ascertained from the current circumstances as there is still much we don't know.

Firstly, we can establish that he is a white male in his thirties or forties. He's efficient with technology due to his ability to remain anonymous throughout e-mails, text messages and phone calls with this victims. He may work in the IT industry, and given his skills with technology, we can assume he possesses a reasonable level of intelligence.

Because of this level of intelligence, we can then deduce that the killer is most likely a psychopath as opposed to a sociopath. That is to say that the killer is an organised offender whose crimes are planned out meticulously beforehand. This also means that he takes great care in order to remove all traces of himself from crime scenes and, judging by the fact he has remained uncaptured for almost twenty years, has achieved this successfully.

The killer's *modus operandi* is entirely unknown. We do not know how he approaches his victims or the circumstances leading up to their initial meeting. Reports from the housemate of Amber Lynn Costello claim that Costello first spoke to the LISK by phone before disappearing to meet him (and was never heard from again). He also said that when Amber spoke to the LISK, they spoke as if they had known each other for a while.

If this is true, this suggests that the LISK is able to charm his victims and lure them into a false sense of security. This would be likely if he is indeed an organised psychopath (similar to Ted Bundy), however, there exists the possibility that Costello and the LISK *did* know each other, or at the very least had met before. Costello's housemate further claimed that the LISK managed to successfully convince Costello to leave her phone at home when they met, a sign of incredible manipulative prowess.

The way in which the LISK disposes of his victims suggests one of two things. Either, he feels remorse for his actions and his subconsciously burying his guilt, or he is concealing their whereabouts as a forensic countermeasure. Given his organised demeanour, it is much more likely to be the latter.

Due to the majority of the discovered victims being females in their twenties, we can assume that he is heterosexual. There are discrepancies in this theory given that there is one male torso and one child torso. However, both can be accounted for with relative ease.

Firstly, if the LISK is indeed an organised, psychopathic sexual predator, this means that his need to kill is compulsive. He won't be able to stop. Due to the extreme care he takes to make sure he remains uncaptured, the LISK chooses victims who would not draw the least amount of attention if they go missing.

Escorts and prostitutes are the easiest victims because their occupation is transient by nature. They don't have work colleagues, the chances of them having partners is slim (compared to non-escorts), and their trade is done via cash, therefore limiting any kind of paper trail to the killer.

The LISK knows all this, and will therefore stick with this target group throughout. The reason for the male victim is likely that there were no other prostitutes or escorts available at the time he felt the compulsion to commit murder. Therefore, he chose the next best thing: a male prostitute in women's clothing.

The baby can be accounted for due it being the child of one his adult victims. It is possible the escort had her baby with her at the time she met the LISK, and so felt he needed to kill the child too.

The way the child victim was discovered suggests that the LISK received no pleasure from murdering an infant, and only did so in order to tie up loose ends. The baby was discovered wrapped in a blanket with no wounds to speak of. The child's cause of death is unknown.

There have been no suspects in the LISK case which have been made known to the general public. There is a possibility that some of the remains uncovered may be the work of serial killer Joel Rifkin. Four of Rifkin's victims were never discovered, and he was a known user of prostitutes in the Long Island area. Rifkin was incarcerated in 1994 for a series of murders, and has been questioned on the subject of the newly-discovered bodies. Rifkin denies any knowledge of them.

Exactly how the LISK has managed to remain uncaptured despite a twenty-year reign of terror in the modern age is a difficult question to answer. The LISK is a mystery which authorities are light-years away from answering.

The closest the police have come to finding the elusive killer was in 2009 when NYPD officers claimed to have spoken to the killer by phone. Just how this situation managed to come about has not been made public knowledge, however, rumours state that such a phone call was at the demands of the killer, not the authorities.

This would be a reasonable assumption, given what we already know about the case. It's highly likely the LISK will remain uncaptured forever and become a future enigma, as other historical uncaught

murders have before him. The case has since
gone cold in the six years since the discovery
of additional bodies, and there appears to be
no advancements.

The Long Island Serial Killer has escaped
justice for twenty years, and likely will for
twenty more.

Part 5 - The Lake Bodom Murders

Finland, 1960. The homicides which took
place at Lake Bodom remain one of Finland's
greatest mysteries. The case was widespread
across Scandinavia and has become one of
the most researched cold cases in the
country's history. While the rest of the world
may be unfamiliar with the incidents which

occurred there, the murders left its mark in Finnish culture.The Lake Bodom murders have inspired multiple television shows, movies, books, theories, blogs and even a heavy metal band.

Lake Bodom is a lake near the city of Espoo, around 20 miles from Helsinki. On 5th June 1960, a group of teenagers went camping on the shores of the lake. In the early hours of the morning, three of them were murdered while they slept in their tents. The killer remains uncaptured to this day.

The reason for the case's infamy lies in the questions which seemingly lead nowhere. The weapon which was used to kill the group cannot be determined, there is no traces of the murderer left behind, and despite confessions from multiple sources, all of which have led nowhere.

The camping group was made up of two couples: Seppo Boisman (M) and Tuulikki Mäki (F), and Nils Gustafsson (M) and Irmeli Björklund (F). The males were eighteen years old, and the females were fifteen years old.

The couples set their tents up in the early evening on the shores of Lake Bodom. At 10:30pm, both couples retired to bed. What happened between the hours of 10:30pm and 6am is largely unknown. The only thing we can ascertained definitely happened was that a fifth party attacked all four members of the group, leaving three of them for dead.

The group was discovered around 11am the following morning by a man jogging across the lake. The police were alerted, and what they discovered was very strange.

It appeared as though whoever had attacked the group had done so from outside their tents. He had blitz attacked them through the tent fabric and done so chaotically. When the group were discovered, all of them possessed multiple stab wounds and were lying in their tents, aside from Nils Gustafsson who was found outside his tent and lying on top of it.

Gustafsson would be the only survivor of the assault, although he received multiple fractures, broken bones and a concussion.

Unfortunately, this is all that has ever been made public knowledge regarding the attack itself. Little else is known. Several items belonging to the group were stolen, notably clothes and money. No murder weapon has ever been discovered in relation to the crimes, and investigators aren't even certain what weapon was used to carry out the killings. Some of the items of clothing which were missing from the campsite were found around 500 yards away, all of which were covered in blood.

Gustafsson's account of the night is limited due to his claims of being attacked first. He says he was disoriented and believed that the killer, whoever it may have been, believed Gustafsson to be dead while he attacked the rest of the group.

Over the years there have been multiple suspects in the Lake Bodom murders, some of which have even confessed to the killings in private. However, the Lake Bodom case is unique in that despite multiple suspects actually confessing, each of them had solid alibis for their whereabouts on the night of the murders.

The first suspect, Pentti Soininen, was a violent criminal who claimed responsibility for the murders to a fellow inmate in his prison in the mid-1960s. It is true that Soininen lived near the murder site, however, he would have been fourteen years old at the time. It is very unlikely one fourteen year old could overpower four similarly aged persons, let alone do it and leave no trace evidence of himself behind.

In a very strange predicament, Pentti Soininen hanged himself in 1969 – on the day of the ninth anniversary of the murders.

Valdemar Gyllstrom was the police's most viable suspect. According to reports, Gyllstrom confessed to the murders to his neighbour while he was intoxicated, although he later denied doing so. Gyllstrom was known as a spiteful man with an unfounded hatred of children and campers.

Several days after the murder, Gyllstrom was seeing pouring concrete into a well in his back garden. Some researchers believe that Gyllstrom may have disposed of the murder weapons (and items of property belonging to the victims) and filled the well in order to hide them.

Strangely, Gyllstrom's wife would provide his alibi for the night of the murders. She claimed that Gyllstrom was in bed all night.

Gyllstrom's involvement could be ascertained much further as, similar to Pentti Soininen, Gyllstrom also committed suicide in 1969. He drowned himself in Lake Bodom.

Amateur researchers believe Hans Assmann, a reported KGB spy was the culprit behind the Lake Bodom massacre. On 6th June 1960, Assmann arrived at the Helsinki Surgical Hospital in an extremely deluded state. His clothes appeared to be blotted with red stains, he was speaking incoherently and his fingernails appeared to be dirtied black.

At points, Assmann pretended he was unconscious in order to manipulate the doctors into seeing him quicker than the other patients. When this didn't work, Assmann became hostile towards staff and patients in the surrounding area and was subsequently told to leave.

It is interesting to note that on the morning of the Lake Bodom murders, two children claimed to have seen a "blonde man" fleeing the crime scene around 6am – the time that the murders were thought to have been committed. Although the children were around ten years old, their claims cannot be discounted.

Assmann, it turns out, had long blonde hair at the time of the murders. When they became widely publicised, Assmann was reported to have shaved off his hair completely bald. Additionally, the clothing which Assmann wore when he entered the hospital that morning matched the description given by the children.

Assmann lived in the Lake Bodom area, and his behaviour around the time of the murders suggested he was hiding something. Many detectives at the time believed Assmann to be involved the killings somehow, even if he wasn't directly responsible. His motive seemed non-existent, however, yet this was the only inconsistency with the theory.

Furthermore, Assmann had been a murder suspect in the past. Second only to the Lake Bodom murders, the case of Auli Kyllikki Saari is one of the most famous cases in Finnish history. It involves the murder of a 17-year-old Finnish girl in 1953 of which Assmann was a major suspect. He was also linked to at least three other unsolved cases. Unfortunately for police, Assmann had an alibi for the night of the murder.

The most interesting suspect, however, is the one survivor of the attack: Nils Gustafsson.

After the incident, Gustafsson lived a normal life for over forty years. He married, had two children and retired. However, in 2004, Finnish police re-opened the case based on new DNA evidence they had discovered.

What police found was blood samples from each of the victims on Gustafsson's shoes. The theory which police put forward was that Gustafsson erupted in a jealous rage over an incident with his new girlfriend, Irmeli Björklund. There are no specific details given as to why Gustafsson would explode in such a manner, but re-examination of the case was authorised based on the new evidence and a possible motive.

In order to explain why Gustafsson had also suffered multiple wounds, police put forward the theory that Gustafsson stabbed and bruised himself in order to make it look as though another perpetrator was responsible.

While it is true that it was Gustafsson's girlfriend Björklund who suffered the most stab wounds, therefore suggesting a personal vendetta, it is unlikely that Gustafsson would be driven to such extremes by mere teenage jealously. In October 2005, Gustafsson was acquitted of all charges, thus rendering the identity of the true killer a mystery.

For over fifty years, the children of Finland have been told to behave themselves for fear that the Bodom murderer will get them. It has become somewhat of a boogeyman in Finland; an almost-supernatural figure who attacks from the shadows without ever being noticed. For a brief moment, the country clung on to the possibility that perhaps this boogeyman may finally be unmasked, but their hopes were dashed and the killer remains free.

As of 2017, most people involved with the mysterious Lake Bodom murders have passed on, taking what little knowledge of the incident they have to their graves. The killer will most likely never be brought to justice, and the question of who brutally murdered three teenagers fifty years ago will go unanswered for eternity.

Conclusion

There is something in the mystery of an unsolved case that really stimulates the imagination. Since the days of Jack the Ripper nearly 130 years ago, amateur and professional researchers alike regularly become immersed in cases in an attempt to unearth the truth, even if that truth takes decades to uncover.

However, we must remember that with mystery comes injustice. For every cold case out there is a criminal who should be punished for their actions. These culprits then, whether they be gangsters, terrorists, serial killers or scorned lovers, can truly be said to have got away with murder.

It is the mystery of these unsolved crimes which amplify their status in the collective conscious. By all accounts, the crimes of Jack the Ripper can be said to be mundane in comparison to more well-known killers of whom their identity has been confirmed.

Jack the Ripper killed a mere five women at most, while killers like Arthur Shawcross, Joel Rifkin and Herbert Mullin killed triple this amount, yet it is the Ripper that becomes a figure of legend due to the allure of an unsolved enigma which he embodies.

Whichever side of the fence you may sit on regarding the existence of unsolved mysteries, such cases are becoming less and less with modern advancements. As you may have noticed in the above, many mysteries are rooted in the past due to our lack of technical and forensic know-how fifty, sixty, seventy years ago.

However, with modern advances comes more opportunities to catch suspects, and with catching suspects come less mysteries. This can only be a good thing because, as evident from the crimes mentioned in this volume, the world has enough mysteries to keep us going for a long time.

Printed in Great Britain
by Amazon